The White Phantom

A Mystery Play in One Act

by Wilbur Braun

A SAMUEL FRENCH ACTING EDITION

SAMUEL FRENCH

FOUNDED 1830

New York Hollywood London Toronto

SAMUELFRENCH.COM

THE WHITE PHANTOM

STORY OF THE PLAY

Perhaps the most attractive feature of this thrill-ing mystery play, aside from its unique plot, is that it can be produced on a platform with just a black cyclorama or black draperies in lieu of scenery. No furniture is necessary since the action of the play takes place in an empty room. Mrs. Drexel Blake, who has social ambitions, rents the old-fashioned residence belonging to The Kingsley Estate. She is preparing to move in on the morrow and is waiting for Eleven Moore, her colored maid, who is coming to help with the cleaning. Eleven is late, and while waiting for her to put in an appearance the lights go out, pistol shots are heard and all sorts of weird happenings occur. Attracted by the unusual noises, Officer Jerry Nolan arrives and takes charge. He attributes the strange occurrences to "The White Phantom," a notorious criminal who is terrorizing the neighborhood. Eleven finally arrives and is left in the living room to put it in order when suddenly she is confronted by the ghostly figure of "The White Phantom" himself. This is one of the funniest scenes ever written into a play! When she is able to relate what has happened to Officer Nolan, Eleven puts the latter on the track of "The Phantom." All clues lead to Curt Frazier, who is in love with Mrs. Blake's charming daughter, Marion. Is he "The Phantom"? The suspense is tense and gripping, and there are more thrills in this one-act play than in the usual three-act play. The final denouement will amaze and interest you, and the play is packed with howls of merriment. That, coupled with the fact that it is so easy to present, has made "The White Phantom" one of the most popular one-act plays ever offered for amateur consumption.

CAST OF CHARACTERS

Mrs. Drexel Blake, *a determined woman.*
Marion Blake, *her young and charming daughter.*
Eleven Moore, *a colored maid.*
Mrs. Ogden Frazier, *a society matron.*
Curtis Frazier, *her son.*
Ethan Sharp, *a real estate man.*
Officer Jerry Nolan, *who means to find out.*
The White Phantom—????

The entire action of the play takes place in the living room of the unoccupied Kingsley residence in an Eastern suburban town.

Time: *The present. An evening in mid-summer.*

DESCRIPTION OF CHARACTERS

MRS. DREXEL BLAKE: *She is the typical society matron. About forty-five years of age, portly, with a will of her own and a frank manner of speaking.*

OFFICER JERRY NOLAN: *He is a policeman. Tall, raw-boned, not too alert in manner, inclined to be blustery in his speech.*

MARION BLAKE: *A charming and pretty girl in her late teens. She is refined in manner and is obviously of good breeding.*

ELEVEN MOORE: *A colored girl in her early teens. She is very small for her age and appears to be younger than she is. Her face is coal black. Her kinky black hair is worn in a braid down her back and tied with a huge bow of ribbon. Her speech reflects the true darkey and she has all of the characteristics of a negress.*

MRS. FRAZIER: *An affected matron, a social climber, the sort of woman who never has a natural moment.*

CURTIS FRAZIER: *A manly, fine-appearing boy in his early twenties. He is gentlemanly in bearing, possessed of a likeable personality.*

ETHAN SHARP *A medium-sized man in his early forties.*

The White Phantom

SCENE: *The living room of the unoccupied Kingsley residence in an Eastern suburban town.*

TIME: *An evening in mid-summer.*

DESCRIPTION OF SET: *This setting can easily be done in draperies if so desired. It is a large, spacious, high-ceilinged room devoid of furniture. A wide arch in rear wall, Center, is the general entrance; interior backing. This arch leads to a hallway. Through the arch and off Right, leads to the front door; through the arch and off Left, leads to the upstairs and other parts of the house. In the Left wall, well downstage, is a door with interior backing. This door leads to the dining room and kitchen. In the Right wall, direct Center, is a fireplace, unlighted. A telephone sits on the floor in extreme upper Right corner. It has a long extension cord. Two large wooden boxes well downstage, one Right of Center and the other Left of Center, are used to sit on. A doorbell ring offstage up Right. The floor and walls are bare as becomes an unoccupied house.*

AT RISE OF CURTAIN: *The stage is in total darkness. After the Curtain has been up a short second, a series of low eerie MOANS are heard, followed by two revolver SHOTS. There is a low mock-*

ing LAUGH in a man's voice, then the DOOR-BELL rings offstage up Right loudly and impatiently. The sound of a wooden BOX being overturned, then another low mocking LAUGH, followed by a babble of confused VOICES. A woman's VOICE is raised in an hysterical shriek, followed by a man's commanding tones cautioning her to keep quiet. Suddenly, without warning, the LIGHTS flash up and disclose MRS. DREXEL BLAKE *and* OFFICER JERRY NOLAN. MRS. BLAKE *stands just below arch Center, an expression of stunned amazement on her face. She is the typical society matron, about forty-five years of age, portly, with a will of her own and a frank manner of speaking. She is dressed in a summer street frock in the latest mode with all accessories of a well-groomed woman.* JERRY *stands just Right of her, looking around the room anxiously. He is a policeman, tall, raw-boned, not too alert in manner, inclined to be blustery in his speech. Wears a conventional blue serge suit, brown shoes with bull dog toes, a white shirt, stiff white collar and a black tie.*

MRS. BLAKE. *(As she looks around bewilderedly)* If you hadn't heard the shots I wouldn't have believed they'd been fired.

JERRY. *(Frowningly)* I heard 'em, all right. Nobody can fool me about shots. *(Turning on her suspiciously)* Who are you, lady?

MRS. BLAKE. *(Turning to him haughtily)* I'm Mrs. Drexel Blake. My husband is connected with the Chamber of Commerce, as was his father before him.

JERRY. *(Disgustedly)* I don't care anythin' 'bout your husband's father, lady. I'm just tryin' to get to the bottom o' this. *(Suspiciously)* What were you doin' 'round here at this time o' night?

MRS. BLAKE. *(Angrily)* Well, I like that! What was I doing indeed! I've rented this house from Mr. Sharp, the real estate man, and I arranged to meet Eleven here tonight so that—

JERRY. *(Interrupting her quickly)* Eleven? Who's that? One o' them public enemies? Are you in cahoots with a crowd o' gangsters?

MRS. BLAKE. *(Coming down C. to R. of wooden box L.C.; indignantly)* If my husband were here you wouldn't dare insult me in this manner.

JERRY. *(Coming to R. of her)* I ain't int'rested in your husband, ma'am. I guess he has troubles o' his own. *(In thundering tones)* Who's this Number Eleven? Come on, out with it! You might as well make a full confession now. I'll find out anyhow.

MRS. BLAKE. *(Drawing herself up to her full height; haughtily)* Eleven is my colored maid. She comes of such a large family that after the fifth child was born they started giving them numbers instead of names. *(Sarcastically)* Does that satisfy you?

JERRY. *(Suspiciously)* Why did they call this one Number Eleven?

MRS. BLAKE. *(Sarcastically)* Because she was born after the tenth child, thereby making her the eleventh. I presume that you can count? *(Crosses to door L. and opens same, looking off anxiously.)*

JERRY. *(Angrily)* You ain't goin' to get no place by mockin' me, ma'am. I represent the Law.

MRS. BLAKE. *(Turning on him angrily)* How do I know you're telling me the truth? How do I know that you are a policeman? Where's your uniform?

JERRY. *(Crossing to fireplace and bending down to inspect same)* My uniform's at the Station House, o' course. I've been detailed to watch this house an' see who's responsible for the goin's on in here. The Captain assigned me to plain-clothes duty.

MRS. BLAKE. *(Closing the door and crossing to* C., *where she faces him; frigidly)* And is that the reason you were sleeping on the front steps as I came along?

JERRY. *(Straightening up and facing her; sheepishly)* I wasn't sleepin', lady. I just seemed to be. Er—you see, I figured it all out by myself that if I closed my eyes an' made out like I was asleep whoever was hidin' in this house'd be caught.

MRS. BLAKE. *(Haughtily)* It was certainly a perfect imitation. If you really are a policeman working in plain clothes—

JERRY. *(Interrupting her quickly)* Say, don't you believe me?

MRS. BLAKE. *(Looking directly at him; emphatically)* I most certainly do. The last policeman on this beat had the same vacant expression on his face that you have and he was just as futile.

JERRY. *(Taking a step toward her; angrily)* Say, lissen—

MRS. BLAKE. *(Breaking in on him quickly)* He was shot to death the third night he worked on this beat. I hope you don't meet with a similar fate—it's such a messy way to die! *(With a complete change of tone; anxiously)* How do you account for the fact, Officer, that when I left this place early this afternoon the door was locked? I know because I tried it to make certain that nobody could get in. Just now, when you turned the front door knob, it opened immediately.

JERRY. *(Blankly)* Now, who d'you s'pose done that?

MRS. BLAKE. *(Frigidly)* I wouldn't know. Aren't you supposed to ascertain such things? *(With pretended sweetness)* I wonder if it would be asking too much of you to search the house? In that way we might determine who is hiding here and why.

JERRY. *(Loudly; in his most blustery manner)* I'll search the house all right in my own good time.

Mrs. Blake. *(Crossing to wooden box* L.C. *and sitting)* Oh, there's no hurry, Officer. Just wait as long as you please. If I had known you were going to visit here I'd have had Eleven bake a cake and bring the tea things over. *(Casts a sarcastic glance at him.)*

Jerry. *(Vacantly)* I don't drink tea. Besides, I ain't got time for such things. I gotta find out what's causin' every tenant to move outa this house no sooner than they move into it. *(Crossing up to barrel and peering into it, then coming down* R. *of her)* So, you've rented this place, eh? Ain't you afraid to move into it?

Mrs. Blake. *(Ironically)* Why should I be when we have such big, brave policemen to protect us?

Jerry. *(Inflating his chest proudly)* Right you are, ma'am. If anybody bothers you I'll nab 'em before they can say Jack Robinson. Nobody ain't gonna put nothin' over on Jerry Nolan, even if I do say it myself.

(The White Phantom *appears in arch* c., *from* R. *He is a medium-sized man, his entire body being covered by a large white sheet that has holes slit in the top for his eyes. White cotton gloves cover his hands. The bottom of his trousers may be seen below the sheet. They are of white linen or palm beach and his feet are encased in white canvas shoes. He hesitates in arch* c. *Unobserved by* Jerry *or* Mrs. Blake, *withdraws quickly* c., *to* L.)

Mrs. Blake. *(Rising quickly)* I can't understand where Eleven is. She'll have to work here all night to get this place clean. I'm moving in tomorrow.

Jerry. *(Curiously)* In spite o' them shots an' all the noises we heard?

Mrs. Blake. *(Resolutely)* Now, you sound exactly like Drexel, my husband. He's been arguing with me for three days, ever since I signed the lease, against taking the place. And the more he argues against moving in here the more determined I am to occupy this house.

JERRY. *(Shaking his head sorrowfully)* My wife's the same way, ma'am. She does all my thinkin' for the both o' us. I guess all women's alike.

MRS. BLAKE. *(Tossing her head energetically)* And it's lucky for you men that we are.

JERRY. *(Crossing to box R.C. and sitting)* Mary keeps tellin' me that, too. She's forever tellin' me how much better off I am since we was married. Not that I'm complainin'. She's a fine gal, all right. There wasn't a prettier gal in this town than Mary Hall was when I married her.

MRS. BLAKE. *(Surprisedly)* You married Mary Hall? The girl who used to go out sewing by the day? Why, I knew her well before she was married.

JERRY. *(Solemnly)* That's where you had the advantage over me, ma'am. I thought I knew her but I didn't. *(Rising)* Well, I s'pose I'd better have a look 'round this place. Them was certainly shots we heard an' I thought I heard somebody groan.

MRS. BLAKE. *(Anxiously)* Don't you think you'd better telephone to the Station and have them send somebody over in case you are shot in the back while you are inspecting the house?

JERRY. *(Nervously)* Why—er—I guess there ain't no danger o' that, ma'am. *(Hastily)* I guess I will phone to Headquarters, though, to let 'em know what's goin' on here. *(Crossing to telephone)* Is this thing connected?

MRS. BLAKE. *(Emphatically)* Oh, yes, I saw to that. I wouldn't move into any house before the telephone was in working order. The men installed it this afternoon.

JERRY. *(Picking up telephone)* Hello—hello— *(He waits a short second, then tries again, shouting.*

There is no response. He jiggles the hook up and down, shouts "Hello," then hangs up disgustedly) I can't get Central nohow. It must be outa order. *(He replaces telephone on floor and comes to* R. *of* MRS. BLAKE.)

MRS. BLAKE. *(Firmly)* That telephone was working late this afternoon. I know because I called Drexel up and gave him the list of things I wanted him to bring home for dinner.

JERRY. *(Decisively)* Well, it ain't workin' now. I'll guarantee that. That telephone is as dead as a Vice President's trap *after* he's elected. *(TELEPHONE rings sharply.)*

MRS. BLAKE. *(Jumps up as though she had been shot, rushes to telephone and picks it up. Speaking into phone)* Hello— Hello— *(Loudly and excitedly)* Hello— I insist on getting Central— I want you to get my husband at once—

JERRY. *(As he crosses to* L. *of her; hastily)* What number?

MRS. BLAKE. *(Turning on him angrily)* Sir? How many husbands do you think I have? The idea! *(She jiggles the hook up and down on telephone; calls again. No response. Hangs up angrily and replaces telephone on floor)* It's no use. I can't get Central to answer.

JERRY. *(Complacently)* I told you the phone ain't workin'.

MRS. BLAKE. *(Demandingly)* Then how do you account for the fact that it rang only a few seconds ago?

JERRY. *(Resolutely)* I don't know, but I mean to find out. *(Crossing to door* L.*)* I'll start to look the place over now. *(*MRS. BLAKE *comes down* C. *He opens the door, then turns to her nervously)* Er—you sure you ain't afraid to stay here alone?

MRS. BLAKE. *(Decisively)* Don't worry about me. I'm not afraid of anything. *(He starts to exit. Her voice stops him)* By the way, Officer, what is your address? Just in case you should be shot and killed, I'd have to know where to send your remains.

JERRY. *(Closing the door quickly)* Er—maybe I'd better look upstairs first. *(He crosses up to arch.)*

MRS. BLAKE. *(Anxiously)* Who do you think is up there?

JERRY. *(His chest inflated; courageously)* I don't know but I mean to find out! *(He exits C., to L.)*

(MRS. BLAKE crosses to box L.C. and is about to sit when the DOORBELL rings. She crosses up; exits C., to R. THE WHITE PHANTOM enters from door L., carrying a letter in a sealed envelope. He crosses to fireplace, laughs mockingly and crosses L., where he exits.)

MRS. BLAKE. *(Just outside of arch; reprovingly)* Marion, why did you have to come over here? Didn't I tell you to stay at home? *(She enters C., from R., her arm around the waist of MARION BLAKE, a charming and pretty girl in her late teens. She is refined in manner and is obviously of good breeding. Her summer frock of organdy is made in the latest fashion and is vastly becoming. Shoes and stockings match her frock and she carries a smart-looking purse.)*

MARION. *(Nervously)* Don't scold me, Mumsey. I just had to come over. It's so lonesome at home with nothing to do. *(They come down C., MRS. BLAKE L. of MARION.)*

MRS. BLAKE. *(Withdrawing her arm from around MARION's waist and surveying her critically)* Marion, have you been crying again?

MARION. *(Nervously)* Why—er—no, that is—I mean—

MRS. BLAKE. *(Breaking in on her quickly)* You

have! And after you promised me that you'd never even think of Curtis Frazier again.

MARION. *(Tearfully)* I try not to, but oh, Mumsey, I'm so unhappy.

MRS. BLAKE. *(Scornfully)* Unhappy over a man? You must have taken leave of your senses. Why, my Aunt Sophia had *never been kissed by a man* when she died at the age of fifty.

MARION. If she'd never been kissed by a man she couldn't have died.

MRS. BLAKE. *(Bewilderedly)* And why not?

MARION. *(With conviction)* Because nothing can die unless it has lived! *(Summoning all her courage)* Mother, why are you so opposed to Curt? If you'd only give me some logical reason for disliking him I'd—

MRS. BLAKE. *(Breaking in quickly)* I've given you a logical reason, Marion. I don't like his mother.

MARION. *(Tearfully)* B-but that's not C-Curt's fault. We can't pick our p-parents.

MRS. BLAKE. *(Furiously)* Marion Blake, is that meant to be a reflection on *your* mother?

MARION. *(Hastily)* Oh, Mumsey, of course not. You know that I adore you and Dad. But Curt is the sweetest thing and we love each other so!

MRS. BLAKE. *(Sharply)* Humph! I've no use for any of that Frazier tribe! The way that Annie Frazier tries to be the social leader of this town is entirely beyond my endurance.

MARION. *(Crossing to box R.C. and sitting; protestingly)* But you and Mrs. Frazier used to be such close friends.

MRS. BLAKE. *(Contemptuously)* Oh, I'll admit that I allowed her to pull the wool over my eyes for some time. I even called her Anastasia just to please her when I knew all the while that her name was really Annie.

MARION. *(Curiously)* Why did you quarrel so suddenly?

MRS. BLAKE. *(Angrily)* There wasn't anything sudden about it. I *just happened* to be present one day without her knowing it. Your father was showing her a new letter-opener that had been given him for a present when Annie Frazier chirped up and said: "You'll have little use for that in this house, Drexel. Your wife is letter-opener enough for any home." *(Taps the floor with point of her foot angrily.)*

MARION. *(Helplessly)* But—

MRS. BLAKE. *(Continuing; ragefully)* Do you think I'd let you have that woman for a mother-in-law? I should say not. Your father still boasts of the fact that when he told Annie Frazier that I talked too much she agreed with him and said that she could have told him so long ago but she didn't want to appear catty.

MARION. *(Bewilderedly)* But Curt—

MRS. BLAKE. *(Furiously)* No wonder she keeps her hair bobbed so short; the coward! *(Rising and taking a step Right, to* MARION*)* I know that she must be having ten fits now that she knows we're moving into this house. For years she's boasted of the fact that she lives in the most select neighborhood in town.

MARION. *(Incredulously)* Is that why you were so determined to move right next door to the Fraziers?

MRS. BLAKE. *(Decisively)* Of course not. *(Crosses back to box and sits)* Nobody is going to lord it over me, Marion. I'll show Annie Frazier that I can be even more grand and elegant than she tries to be.

MARION. *(Nervously)* But, M-Mother, all this has nothing to do with C-Curt and me. We—

MRS. BLAKE. *(Breaking in on her quickly)* Curt is no better than his mother, Marion. Where does he go when he disappears suddenly on these long trips? He's much too mysterious to suit me.

MARION. *(Loyally)* Why, there's nothing mysterious about Curt; nothing at all. He's the very soul of—

MRS. BLAKE. *(Cutting in on her quickly)* Have you asked him where he goes on these trips he's forever taking?

MARION. *(Nervously)* Why—er—I—

MRS. BLAKE. *(Triumphantly)* You did, but he refused to give you any information. He's exactly like his mother. Annie Frazier always wants to know everybody else's business but will never divulge any of her own.

MARION. *(Rising; impatiently)* But, Mother, Curt has a perfect right to live his own life without any interference from me.

MRS. BLAKE. *(Angrily)* Oh, he has, eh?

MARION. Of course. Didn't Father have **any** secrets from you *before* you were married?

MRS. BLAKE. *(Rising; determinedly)* He *thought* he did, my dear—he knows better now than to even *try* to conceal anything from me. *(Triumphantly)* Your Dad knows that even if he ventures to *mumble* in his sleep I can tell him the next day exactly what he said!

(JERRY *appears in arch and starts down* C.)

MARION. *(Tearfully)* If I can't marry Curt I'll stay single the rest of my life.

MRS. BLAKE. *(Turning and seeing* JERRY) Well, Officer, did you find anybody? *(She faces him anxiously.* JERRY *stands between* MARION *and* MRS. BLAKE, *the latter* L. *of him.)*

MARION. *(Astonishedly)* Why, Mother, what is an Officer doing here?

MRS. BLAKE. *(Disgustedly)* The same thing they're

always doing—loafing. *(DOORBELL rings.)* See who that is, Marion.

JERRY. *(Angrily)* I'll answer the bell. Loafin', eh? That sounds just like my wife. *(Crosses up to arch, muttering as he goes)* You can't please women folks. They're all alike. *(He exits* C., *to* R.*)*

MARION. *(Anxiously)* What is he doing here, Mother?

MRS. BLAKE. *(Crossing* L. *to just below wooden box)* It's nothing, Marion. He's just inspecting the premises before we move in.

MARION. *(Fearfully)* You mean there have been more disturbances here? *(Pleadingly)* Oh, Mother, I do wish you'd give up the idea of moving into this house. *(*ELEVEN MOORE, *a colored girl in her early teens, appears* C. *from* R. *She is very small for her age and appears to be younger than she is. Her face is coal black. Her kinky black hair is worn in a braid down her back and tied with a huge bow of ribbon. Her speech reflects the true darkey and she has all of the characteristics of a negress. A boy's cap covers her head and her calico dress is of a loud color done in checks or stripes. She presents a comic appearance as she hesitates in arch, an empty cleaning pail in one hand and three or four cleaning cloths in the other.)* Everybody in town says that this place is *haunted!* *(*ELEVEN *utters a loud scream and drops the empty pail to the floor, her knees trembling violently.* MAR-ION *crosses* R. *to front of fireplace.* JERRY *enters quickly* C., *from* R., *and appears in arch.)*

MRS. BLAKE. *(Crossing up to* L. *of* ELEVEN*)* Eleven Moore, you're late. You should have been here an hour ago!

ELEVEN. *(Nervously)* W-why? W-what's bin h-happenin'?

MRS. BLAKE. *(Commandingly)* Pick that pail up. Stand still.

Eleven. *(Tremblingly)* Ah ain't movin', Mis' Blake. Ah jist 'pears tuh be.

Mrs. Blake. *(Angrily)* Did you hear what I said? Pick that pail up off the floor. (Jerry *stands* R. *of* Eleven, *eyeing her intently.)*

Eleven. *(Fearfully)* Yassum, Ah heerd yuh all, Mis' Blake, but mah body don't seem willin' tuh follow your direcshuns. *(She reaches down slowly, as though with great effort, picks up the pail and heaves a sigh of relief when she straightens up. Turns and sees* Jerry, *then rolls her eyes wide with fright and faces* Mrs. Blake) Who's him?

Jerry. *(Thunderingly)* I'm a policeman, that's who I am.

Eleven. *(Loudly and fearfully)* Oh, please, Mister Officer, I ain't done nuthin'. Neither has mah Pappy. He done 'splain to de Judge how he come to have dat chicken in his possession.

Jerry. *(Triumphantly)* Aha! So your father stole a chicken, did he?

Eleven. *(Earnestly)* No, suh, Mister Officer, mah Pappy didn't steal dat chicken. Yuh see, we done had de eggs an' mah Pappy thought it war a shame tuh separate de parents from de offspring so he jist brought dat chicken home wit' him.

Mrs. Blake. *(Crossing down to below wooden box)* Where have you been all this time, Eleven? You'll have to stay here and work all night.

Eleven. *(Coming down* C. *to* R. *of her.* Jerry *follows her down to* R. *of* Eleven. Marion *stands in front of fireplace.)* Ah's feered Ah ain't up tuh much work dis evenin', Mis' Blake, ma'am. Ah jist come from de doctor.

Mrs. Blake. *(Incredulously)* The doctor? Do you expect me to believe that?

Eleven. Dat's mah story an' Ah'm stuck with it.

Marion. *(Sympathetically)* Did the doctor take your temperature, Eleven?

ELEVEN. *(Turning to* MARION) Ah don't know as to dat, Mis' Marion, ma'am. All Ah's missed so far is mah han'kerchief.

JERRY. *(Thunderingly)* What made you scream just now when you dropped that pail?

ELEVEN. *(Turning to him nervously)* Ah guess yuh all'd scream too if somebody tol' you dat dis house wuz ha'nted. All de folks what moves into dis place done moved right out. Dat Mis' Johnson, what lived here last, sez she seed a white ghost movin' here every evenin'.

JERRY. *(Contemptuously)* Well, there ain't any ghosts here, you can be sure of that. *(Inflating his chest; proudly)* You've got nothing to worry about while Jerry Nolan is on the job.

(Three distinct TAPS are heard off L. ELEVEN *falls on her knees in a praying attitude, dropping the empty pail and the cleaning cloths on the floor beside her.)*

MARION *and* MRS. BLAKE. *(Together; fearfully)* What's that?

JERRY. *(Importantly)* I don't know, but I mean to find out! *(Rushes to door* L., *opens same quickly and peers off.)*

ELEVEN. *(Her teeth chattering with fear)* O-oh, L-Lord, s-save l-little 'L-Leven f-from de e-evil s-spirits.

MRS. BLAKE. *(Crossing* R. *to* MARION ; *turning and facing* ELEVEN ; *commandingly)* Stop that this instant.

JERRY. *(Turning and facing her)* Now, you lissen to me, lady. I'm in charge here an' I have to do my work as I see fit.

MRS. BLAKE. *(Frigidly)* I was speaking to my maid. Might I suggest, Officer, that you go out there and see who is causing this disturbance or would it be too much trouble?

JERRY. *(Irritably)* I'm on my way out there now. Remember, nobody is to leave here 'til I get back. *(Exits quickly L.)*

MRS. BLAKE. *(To ELEVEN)* Get up off the floor and start cleaning these walls. I want this house spic and span before I move into it.

ELEVEN. *(Wailingly)* 'Tain't no use fer me to clean it, Mis' Blake, 'cause dat ghostes am only gwine tuh dirty it all up again.

MRS. BLAKE. *(Furiously)* Do you want this job, or don't you?

ELEVEN. *(Nervously)* No'm. Er—Ah means yassum. Ah's dat jittery Ah kain't git mah tongue tuh say de right thing. *(She starts praying again)* Dear Lord, don't let dat ghostes git Little 'Leven—   ?

MRS. BLAKE. *(Breaking in on her; angrily)* Get up off that floor and stop that noise.

ELEVEN. *(Rising with a great effort)* Dat ain't noise, Mis' Blake. Dat's Gospel what Ah learned in Sunday School. De teacher taught us dat whiniver we is tempted we should git down on our knees an' pray, even if it's right in de midst o' a watermillion patch. *(Rolls her eyes wide.)*

MRS. BLAKE. *(Querulously)* But you aren't tempted now, Eleven.

ELEVEN. *(Emphatically)* Deed Ah is, Mis' Blake, ma'am. Ah's tempted tuh try tuh reach dat front door an' go right through it!

JERRY. *(As he enters L.; importantly)* There ain't a sign of anybody out there. Those taps musta come from the house next door.

MRS. BLAKE. *(Triumphantly)* For once I agree with you, Officer. Annie Frazier knows that I'm moving in here tomorrow and she's trying to frighten me away.

MARION. *(Earnestly)* Oh, Mother, I think you're

doing Mrs. Frazier a great injustice. She wouldn't be guilty of such a thing.

Mrs. Blake. *(Irritably)* Oh, wouldn't she? I know that woman better than you do, Marion.

Jerry. *(Taking a few steps* R.; *importantly)* I've looked over the whole house an' I'm sure there ain't nobody here but us four, countin' her. *(Points to* Eleven. *All LIGHTS go out suddenly, leaving the stage in inky blackness.* The White Phantom *laughs mockingly just outside door* L. Marion, Eleven *and* Mrs. Blake *shriek wildly. A BODY falls to the floor. A confused babble of voices is heard, mingled with screams and moans.)*

Mrs. Blake. *(Excitedly)* Let go of me, Marion. I can't move my arms!

(All LIGHTS flash up suddenly. Jerry *is lying on the floor just below box* L.C., *his eyes closed.* Marion *stands just below box* R.C., *facing* C. Eleven *is nowhere in sight.* Mrs. Blake *stands* C. *Standing close beside her is* Mrs. Ogden Frazier, *a tall, imposing woman in her late forties. Her arms are fastened around* Mrs. Blake *so that the latter's arms are pinned to her side.* Mrs. Frazier *is an affected matron, a social climber, the sort of woman who never has a natural moment. She is well-groomed and beautifully attired in an evening gown of the latest mode with all accessories to match, and her hair is bobbed very short.)*

Mrs. Frazier. *(Releasing* Mrs. Blake *as the lights flash up)* Oh, it's you! *(She takes a step away from her disappointedly.)*

Mrs. Blake. *(Furiously)* Annie Frazier! What are you doing in *my* house?

Mrs. Frazier. *(Facing her; indignantly)* Well, you may be sure I didn't come to pay you a visit.

Minnie Blake. I thought I had captured The White Phantom!

JERRY. *(Opening his eyes and moaning softly)* What hit me?

MARION. *(Rushing over and bending down R. of him; anxiously)* Are you hurt, Officer?

JERRY. *(Sitting up with a great effort and rubbing the back of his head)* Soon as the lights went out, somebody connected their fist with the back of my head. (MARION *rises.*) I remember now that I smelled some perfumery.

MRS. FRAZIER. *(Crossing R. to fireplace; triumphantly)* The White Phantom! He always uses it. *(To* JERRY*; anxiously)* Was it a sort of sickly odor?

JERRY. *(Irritably)* It didn't smell like roses, I can tell you that.

MARION. *(Rising; solicitously)* Shall I get a doctor to look at your head?

JERRY. *(Rising and rubbing his head)* A doctor couldn't help my head none.

MRS. BLAKE. *(Sarcastically)* Perhaps we'd better send for a carpenter, then. *(Angrily)* If something doesn't happen soon I'm going to insist on sending for the police. (JERRY *takes down extreme* L. MRS. BLAKE *crosses to box* L.C. *and sits.* MARION *crosses to fireplace and just below* MRS. FRAZIER.)

MRS. FRAZIER. *(Decisively)* The police don't seem able to cope with this situation. The White Phantom just sneers at the Law.

JERRY. *(Angrily)* Oh, he does, eh? I'd like to come in contact with him just once.

MRS. BLAKE. *(Frigidly)* You'd be no match for him. He's a master mind.

MRS. FRAZIER. *(In her most affected manner)* I must be getting back to my guests. *(To* JERRY*)* I do hope you are successful in putting an end to the weird happenings in this house, Officer. It's very disturbing, to say the least.

JERRY. *(Feeling the back of his head)* You're telling me!

MRS. FRAZIER. *(Importantly)* I am Mrs. Ogden Frazier, Officer. No doubt you've heard of my husband.

JERRY. *(Greatly awed)* Yes, indeed, ma'am. He's the most important man in this town.

MRS. BLAKE. *(Jumping up quickly)* We're not here to discuss wealth or position, Officer. *(Pointing to MRS. FRAZIER)* Don't let Annie Frazier awe you by her affected manner. She is responsible for everything that has happened here tonight.

MARION. *(Pleadingly)* Mother!

MRS. BLAKE. *(Furiously)* You keep quiet, Marion. This is a serious matter. *(To JERRY)* That woman is trying to frighten me out of this house. She's planned a campaign to make me move away because she doesn't want me in the house next to her.

JERRY. *(Heatedly)* She didn't hit me on the head, did she?

MRS. FRAZIER. *(Smiling at JERRY in her most affected manner)* You are a man of rare intelligence, Officer. I could see that the moment I looked at you. I shall speak to Ogden about you and have him use his influence to have you promoted.

MRS. BLAKE. *(Angrily)* You needn't think you can wiggle out of this by bribing an Officer, Annie Frazier.

MRS. FRAZIER. *(Haughtily)* I'll not stay here and listen to any more insults. *(To JERRY)* You know where to find me if you want me, Officer.

JERRY. *(Making a stiff bow)* Certainly, Mrs. Frazier, ma'am. I'll drop in next door after I've settled things here.

MRS. BLAKE. *(Furiously)* Humph! (MRS. FRAZIER *starts for arch* C. MRS. BLAKE *jumps up quickly and turns to* JERRY) Officer, I insist that that woman be detained here. (MRS. FRAZIER *pauses in arch* C.)

JERRY. *(Bewilderedly)* What for?

MRS. BLAKE. *(Wailingly)* Where's my maid? Somebody has spirited her away!

JERRY. *(Looking around the room anxiously)* That's right. She ain't here. I forgot all about *Thirteen!*

MRS. BLAKE. *(Angrily)* You mean Eleven. Somebody's kidnaped her.

MRS. FRAZIER. *(Taking a step downstage)* Surely you don't think I had anything to do with this, Officer? I could hardly be responsible for the girl's disappearance, especially when I discharged her several months ago.

JERRY. *(Crossing up and standing* L. *of* MRS. FRAZIER) She used to work for you?

MRS. FRAZIER. *(Nodding affirmatively)* Yes, I felt sorry for the poor child and engaged her. But my guests complained about her, so I had to let her go.

MRS. BLAKE. *(Crossing to* L. *of* JERRY; *emphatically)* That isn't so. Eleven came to me and asked me for a position while Annie Frazier was employing her. The poor child complained about not getting enough to eat while she worked in the Frazier house and she left of her own accord.

MRS. FRAZIER. *(Furiously)* The idea! There isn't a word of truth to that tale, Officer. *(The* TWO WOMEN *glare at each other.)*

MARION. *(Trying to pour oil on the troubled waters)* Don't you think you'd better search the house again, Officer?

JERRY. *(Desperately)* But I've been over it, Miss, an' there wasn't no traces of anybody.

MRS. FRAZIER. *(In her most affected manner)* These disturbances have been going on in here for months, Officer. That's why no sane person would even consider moving in. (MARION *turns and inspects the fireplace.*)

JERRY. *(To* MRS. BLAKE) Don't get upset, ma'am. I'll get to the bottom of it if it takes the rest of my life.

MRS. BLAKE. *(Coming to below box* L.C.) It probably will. If you ever do get to the bottom of it you'll find what I told you is true. The Fraziers are responsible for—

MARION. *(Bending down over fireplace; excitedly)* Look! Somebody's left a letter here. (JERRY *rushes over to her. She straightens up, handing the letter to him.)*

MRS. BLAKE. *(Crossing to* C.; *excitedly)* A letter! What does it say? Who is it addressed to? *(She faces* JERRY. MRS. FRAZIER *comes down to back of box* R.C. ALL *eyes intent on* JERRY *and the letter.)*

JERRY. *(Ripping the envelope open and removing the letter, he starts to read same)* "Be warned in time. Death and destruction will be visited upon you if you are found in this house after twelve o'clock this night." (MRS. FRAZIER *screams loudly.* ELEVEN *sticks her head out of barrel up* L., *unobserved by the* OTHERS. *She rolls her eyes wide with fright.)*

MRS. BLAKE. *(Commandingly)* Go on, Officer. What else does it say?

JERRY. *(Continuing to read from the letter)* "It is useless to appeal to the stupid Police. They will not be able to cope with spirits from another world. Leave quietly now and all will be well. Signed: *The White Phantom!"* (ELEVEN *places her hand over her mouth to prevent screaming and ducks back into barrel where she is completely hidden from view.)*

MRS. FRAZIER. *(Triumphantly)* "The White Phantom!" I knew he was at the bottom of this!

MARION. *(Fearfully)* Oh, Mother, let's leave this place at once. It's not safe to remain here. *(She crosses to box* R.C. *and sinks onto same.)*

MRS. BLAKE. *(Crossing to box* L.C. *and sitting, resolutely)* You can all leave if you wish to do so. I'm staying right here, Phantom or no Phantom.

MARION. *(Protestingly)* But, Mother—

MRS. BLAKE. *(Cutting in on her quickly)* Don't argue with your mother, Marion. No doubt your father will be worried about us soon and come over here to get us. *(Looking directly at* JERRY) That's what we need in this house tonight. A man who isn't afraid of his own shadow.

JERRY. *(Crossing to* R. *of* MRS. BLAKE) I ain't afraid o' nothin' or nobody, lady.

MRS. FRAZIER. Nobody could be blamed for fearing The White Phantom, Officer. He has committed the most outrageous crimes. Authorities everywhere have been baffled by him. Some people think he is a ghostly creature from another world. (ELEVEN *groans loudly inside the barrel.)*

MARION. *(Jumping to her feet quickly)* What was that?

JERRY. *(Folding the letter and placing it in trouser pocket)* Er—maybe it was the wind.

MRS. BLAKE. *(Scoffingly)* Wind on a summer night? *(To* MARION) Don't stand there like a dummy, Marion. Do something. Get your father. Get the Police. *(Rising; hysterically)* Are you waiting for us all to be murdered, Officer? I wouldn't put it past the Frazier tribe to kill us all before the night is over.

MRS. FRAZIER. *(Crossing to* C.; *furiously)* One more such remark, Minnie Blake, and I'll start legal proceedings against you for slander. *(Two revolver SHOTS are heard just outside* L.)

MARION. *(Frightenedly)* More pistol shots. *(To* JERRY; *pleadingly)* Who was that?

JERRY. *(Rushing to door* L.) I don't know, but I mean to find out! *(He exits quickly.)*

MRS. BLAKE. *(Hopefully)* Maybe somebody will

shoot that Officer; then we'll be able to get a real policeman.

MARION. *(Nervously)* One is the same as the other. *(Pleadingly)* Oh, Mother, let's get out of here while we can. (ELEVEN *groans loudly.)*

MRS. FRAZIER. *(Startled)* There it is again. I'm leaving here now. *(She starts for arch c.)*

JERRY. *(Just outside of door L.; triumphantly)* Aha! Caught you that time, my fine lad. *(His voice stops MRS. FRAZIER, who hesitates in arch. JERRY enters L., his hand fastened to the arm of CURTIS FRAZIER, a manly, fine-appearing boy in his early twenties. He is gentlemanly in bearing, possessed of a likeable personality. Wears a pair of white trousers, white shoes, a soft white shirt with collar attached, a bright necktie, a dark blue coat; no hat.)*

MRS. FRAZIER *and* MARION. *(Together in startled tones, as they see CURTIS)* Curtis!

JERRY. *(Pausing in front of door L.; joyously)* I got him this time! *(To CURTIS)* So you can put it over on the Police, can you? We'll see about that. *(To MRS. BLAKE)* I told you I'd catch this White Phantom, and here he is.

MRS. FRAZIER. *(Coming down c.; in her haughtiest manner)* Officer, release him at once. That's Curtis Frazier, my son!

JERRY. *(Obstinately)* He may be your son but he's The White Phantom just the same.

MARION. *(Desperately)* But that's absurd. Curt couldn't be The White Phantom. *(She holds a hand out to CURTIS in a pleading gesture.)*

MRS. BLAKE. *(Triumphantly)* And why couldn't he? I've said right along that the Frazier tribe were connected with these crimes.

MRS. FRAZIER. *(Furiously)* Oh!

MRS. BLAKE. *(Happily)* You see, Marion, it all tallies. It accounts for Curtis Frazier's long absences and the mysterious trips he's been taking recently.

MARION. *(To* CURTIS; *pleadingly)* Oh, Curt, say something. Don't stand there silently.

CURTIS. *(Stoutly)* I'll have plenty to say if your mother will only give me an opportunity, Marion. *(To* JERRY) Officer, you've made a grave mistake.

MRS. BLAKE. *(To* JERRY; *emphatically)* Don't allow him to sway you from your duty. Criminals always deny their guilt. *(Excitedly)* Didn't you say that The White Phantom always uses a sickly smelling perfume, Officer?

JERRY. *(Nodding affirmatively)* That's right.

MRS. BLAKE. *(As though exploding a bombshell)* I was in Spillman's drug store the other day when Curtis Frazier came in and whispered with the clerk. I just happened to overhear what they were talking about.

MARION. *(Pleadingly)* Mother, please—

MRS. BLAKE. *(Ignoring her and continuing)* They were discussing a certain perfume that this young man had sent away for. *(Points to* CURTIS *accusingly)* I saw the clerk hand him a bottle.

JERRY. *(To* CURTIS; *loudly)* Is this true?

CURTIS. *(Nervously; lowering his eyes)* Why—er—in a way it is, but—

MRS. BLAKE. *(Enjoying herself hugely)* He gave some of that perfume to my daughter and I threw it out because it had such a terrible smell. I'm sure it's the very odor we detected in this room tonight.

MARION. *(Loyally)* I can explain about that perfume, Officer. Curtis got it because—

CURTIS. *(Breaking in on her quickly)* Marion, I forbid you to say another word.

MRS. FRAZIER. *(Tearfully)* It's just like my boy to be chivalrous and not wish to drag a girl into such an affair in spite of—

MRS. BLAKE. *(Turning and facing her furiously)* My daughter had nothing to do with this White Phantom business, if that's what you're trying to imply.

And it won't do your son any good to try to hide his guilt by pretending that she knew anything about it.

MARION. *(Decisively)* Curt has nothing to hide, Mother. You are misjudging him cruelly.

CURTIS. *(Quietly)* It's all right, Marion. Don't worry. I can take it.

MRS. BLAKE. *(With pretended sweetness)* What is the punishment for this sort of thing, Officer?

JERRY. *(Solemnly)* Life imprisonment, ma'am.

MRS. BLAKE. *(Disappointedly)* Is that all? It hardly seems enough. *(Looking at* MRS. FRAZIER *significantly)* I guess some people won't be so uppity after this becomes known.

CURTIS. *(Sincerely)* Look here, Officer, you have no proof that I am The White Phantom.

JERRY. *(Thunderingly)* No proof, eh? Then what were you doin' out there firin' pistol shots?

CURTIS. *(Stoutly)* I didn't fire any shots. I heard them as I was passing the house and rushed in just as anybody would.

JERRY. *(Brusquely)* A likely story. You were the only person out there.

CURTIS. *(Significantly)* You mean I was the only one that you saw. *(ELEVEN groans loudly.)*

MRS. BLAKE. *(Shiveringly)* There it is again—that awful sound.

MRS. FRAZIER. *(Tearfully)* This would never have happened if you had attended my party this evening as I begged you to, Curtis.

CURTIS. *(Loyally)* I told you I wouldn't attend any party that didn't include Marion, Mother. Besides, my mind wasn't on parties.

JERRY. *(Sneeringly)* I'll say it wasn't. *(Commandingly)* Hold your arms up. *(CURTIS raises his arms above his head. JERRY starts to search him, reaches into CURTIS's trouser pocket and brings forth a pair of white cotton gloves)* Aha! What are these gloves doing in your pocket?

CURTIS. *(Nervously)* Why—I—er—

MRS. BLAKE. *(Triumphantly)* There! You see! He can't answer. Everybody knows that The White Phantom always wears white cotton gloves. (JERRY *holds the gloves up for inspection.)*

MARION. *(Pleadingly)* Speak up, Curt. Tell them the truth. You'll have to make a clean breast of things now.

JERRY. *(Sneeringly)* I suppose you bought these to play golf with, eh?

CURTIS. Of course I didn't buy them. *(To* JERRY; *as though suddenly inspired)* Officer, I'll make a bargain with you. If you'll step outside in the hallway with me I'll tell you everything you want to know.

JERRY. *(Sharply)* Why can't you make your confession here?

CURTIS. *(Nervously)* Why—er—I— *(Hanging his head ashamedly)* You'd hardly make me put my mother through such an ordeal. It will only take a few moments. You've everything to gain and nothing to lose by complying with my request.

JERRY. *(Placing a hand on* CURTIS's *shoulder and leading him up to arch)* All right. But remember, no tricks, young feller. *(To* MRS. BLAKE) Didn't I tell you I'd capture The White Phantom? *(Leads* CURTIS *off* C. *to* R.)

MRS. FRAZIER. *(Sobbingly)* Oh, this is dreadful. My son a criminal! I can't believe it.

MARION. *(Crossing to her and placing an arm around her waist in a soothing manner)* There, there, Mrs. Frazier. Curt isn't a criminal. *(Leads her to box* R.C. *and helps her to sit)* I *know* that he is innocent. *(Stands* L. *of* MRS. FRAZIER.)

MRS. BLAKE. *(Sitting on box* L.C.) Marion, be careful of what you say. You don't *know* anything about this affair, nothing whatsoever.

MARION. *(As she crosses to arch* C.) Curt is

innocent. I do know that. *(Looks off* R.; *excitedly)* Something's wrong. The Officer is lying on the floor unconscious! (MRS. FRAZIER *and* MRS. BLAKE *jump up quickly.)*

MRS. BLAKE. *(As she rushes to arch)* No doubt this is some more of Curtis's villainy.

MARION. *(Excitedly)* I'm going to find out what it is all about. *(She rushes off* C. *to* R., *followed by* MRS. BLAKE *and* MRS. FRAZIER. ELEVEN *sticks her head out of the barrel and glances around the room cautiously. She climbs out of the barrel and starts to sneak up to arch.* THE WHITE PHANTOM *glides on from* L., *pauses just in front of door and hisses softly.* ELEVEN *turns and sees him and falls to the floor on her knees, just below arch* C.)

ELEVEN. *(Her teeth chattering with fear)* P-please, M-Mr. G-Ghostes. Ah ain't d-done n-nothin' w-wrong.

THE WHITE PHANTOM. *(Folding his arms and facing straight out front)* Death and destruction to all unbelievers.

ELEVEN. *(Tremblingly)* Ah's daid an' Ah don't know it.

THE WHITE PHANTOM. *(In low mysterious tones)* Are you an unbeliever?

ELEVEN. Ah don't know what Ah is or where Ah's goin'!

THE WHITE PHANTOM. *(Taking a step toward her)* I am a ghost!

ELEVEN. *(Trying to shrink away from him)* If yuh all come one step nearer Ah'll be a ghostes, too.

THE WHITE PHANTOM. *(Crossing to* L. *of her)* I want you!

ELEVEN. W-what f-fer? If dis keeps up Ah w-won't be n-no g-good to n-nobody.

THE WHITE PHANTOM. *(Extending his arms toward her)* If you follow my orders you *might* live. But if you disobey me it means instant death.

Eleven. *(Tremblingly)* The way Ah feels already Ah's three quarters d-daid an' the other quarter is about to f-follow.

The White Phantom. *(Warningly)* If you don't do as I tell you to, I shall haunt you wherever you go.

Eleven. Ah ain't goin' no place. Mah body jist won't navigate nohow.

The White Phantom. *(Facing straight out front, his arms extended into space)* There is only one thing that can save you.

Eleven. *(Tremblingly)* An' that one thing am beyon' mah reach. It am de front door.

The White Phantom. You cannot escape a spirit.

Eleven. You're tellin' me?

The White Phantom. *(Turning and facing her; impressively)* You must get all of these people out of this house at once. Tell them you've spoken with The White Phantom and that they are taking their lives in their hands by staying here.

Eleven. *(Groaningly)* Ah ain't goin' to have dat much breath lef' even if mah heart does leave mah mouth an' go back down where it belongs.

The White Phantom. *(Soothingly)* You can't die yet!

Eleven. *(Moaningly)* If yuh all felt lahk Ah does right now yuh all'd know Ah kain't do nothin' else but to kick de bucket.

The White Phantom. *(Impressively)* Remember, get rid of all these people and don't let them enter this house ever again. That goes for you, too.

Eleven. Mister Ghostes, does yuh all think Ah's insane? If Ah ever lives to breathe fresh air again, Ah'll never come within a mile o' this place, nohow!

The White Phantom. *(Crossing down to door Left)* Remember, I have warned you. Unless you leave this place and make the rest of these people leave you'll all be dead before morning. The White

Phantom has spoken. *(He laughs mockingly and exits* L.*)*

ELEVEN. *(Rolling her eyes wide with fear)* Oh, please, Lord, let Little 'Leven rise to her feet an' depart. Ah'll never eat another piece o' stolen chicken again. Ah'll never crave no more watermillion—

MRS. BLAKE. *(Entering quickly* C. *from* R., *and coming through arch; astonishedly)* Eleven! Is it really you?

ELEVEN. *(Tremblingly)* No'm. It am jist the shadow o' what Ah used to be.

MRS. BLAKE. *(Crossing to* R. *of her and helping her to rise)* Where have you been?

ELEVEN. *(Clutching her for support)* Ah don't know as to that, ma'am, but it sure wuz powerful cold. (MRS. BLAKE *leads her to box* L.C. *and places her on same. She stands* L. *of box.)*

(MARION, MRS. FRAZIER *and* JERRY *appear in arch from* R. JERRY *is hatless. his hair is disheveled, his necktie is gone and his collar is open at the neck. His right eye is discolored.)*

MRS. FRAZIER. *(As they enter)* I can't believe that Curtis would do such a thing. *(Crosses to box* R.C. *and sits, sobbing softly.)*

JERRY. *(Feeling his eye)* If you had this eye you'd believe it. *(Crosses down* C. MARION *comes down to head of fireplace.)*

MRS. FRAZIER. *(Tearfully)* It all comes of Curtis's fondness for reading crime stories. I warned him to stop reading them but he would persist. *(She sobs softly.)*

MRS. BLAKE. *(Pointing to* ELEVEN) Look, Officer Nolan. She's back.

JERRY. *(In his most blustery manner)* I've got a lotta questions to ask you, Thirteen.

ELEVEN. *(Irritably)* Man, Ah ain't Thirteen. Dat's mah sister. Ah's Eleven.

MARION. *(Anxiously)* Officer, are you *positive* that it was Curtis who hit you?

JERRY. *(Turning to her; furiously)* Am I positive? Can't you see this eye? No sooner had we landed in the hall than he turned and socked me in the eye.

MRS. BLAKE. *(Excitedly)* Go on. What happened then?

JERRY. *(Sheepishly)* When I come to, you ladies was bendin' over me.

MRS. FRAZIER. *(Sobbingly)* I warned him not to read those dreaful mystery stories.

MRS. BLAKE. *(Decisively)* It's plain to see why he hit you, Officer Nolan.

JERRY. *(Groaningly)* It must be plain to see, judgin' from the way this eye feels. The boys at Headquarters will give me an awful razzin'.

MRS. BLAKE. *(Emphatically)* That's the last we'll see of Curtis Frazier in these parts; I'm positive of that. *(To* MARION*)* You've had a lucky escape, daughter.

(CURTIS *appears in arch* C., *unobserved by the* OTHERS. *He looks around the room hastily, then motions off* R. ETHAN SHARP, *a medium-sized man in his early forties, enters quickly* C. *from* R., *and joins* CURTIS *in arch. He wears a pair of white trousers, soft white shirt with collar attached, dark necktie, white shoes, a dark coat; no hat. He stands* R. *of* CURTIS.)

MARION. *(Resolutely)* If the entire world said that Curtis was guilty I would still know that he is innocent!

CURTIS. *(Joyously)* Bully for you, Marion!

(*Those seated rise quickly.* JERRY *rushes up to* L.

of CURTIS *and places a hand on the latter's
shoulder in a firm grip.*)

MRS. FRAZIER *and* MARION. *(Together; astonishedly)* Curt!

JERRY. *(Growling at him loudly)* You're under arrest, feller. It'll go hard with you after what you've done.

ETHAN. *(Smiling pleasantly)* Don't be silly, Officer. You're speaking to the hero of the town, the man who was responsible for capturing The White Phantom.

MRS. BLAKE. *(Astonishedly)* What did you say, Mr. Sharp?

JERRY. *(To* MRS. BLAKE) Do you know this man?

MRS. BLAKE. *(Decisively)* Of course. He's Ethan Sharp, the real estate man. I rented this house from him.

ETHAN. *(Politely)* And you got a bargain, Mrs. Blake. It's a lovely house. So quiet and peaceful.

ELEVEN. *(Indignantly)* Sez you!

ETHAN. *(Pleasantly)* I just heard the good news and hastened over to tell you about it, Mrs. Frazier. when I met Curtis.

MRS. FRAZIER. *(Anxiously)* Is it true, Curt? Did you really capture The White Phantom?

CURTIS. *(Modestly)* It was through my efforts that the Police landed him, Mother. I'll get half the reward—ten thousand dollars. *(He smiles at* MARION, MRS. FRAZIER *crosses to below fireplace.*)

JERRY. *(Bewilderedly)* Is this the truth? Have they really got The White Phantom?

CURTIS. *(Happily)* That's right. He's safe in jail. You see, Officer, that accounts for the bottle of perfume Mrs. Blake saw me get at Spillman's drug store. I was having it analyzed. I only needed a few drops of it so I gave the rest to Marion.

MARION. *(Earnestly)* It also accounts for Curt's mysterious absences, Mother. He was on the trail of The White Phantom, but he didn't want anybody to know it. He's been working on this case for months.

MRS. BLAKE. *(Turning to* CURTIS; *affectedly)* Well, I must say I think it was real mean of you not to tell me, Curt. You might have known I'd never say a word to anybody. *(She sits on box* L.C. ELEVEN *is* L. *of her.)*

CURTIS. *(Crossing* R. *to* MARION) I was afraid to tell anybody but Marion about my ambition to get that reward, or at least part of it. I knew I could trust her.

JERRY. *(Exasperatedly)* You get the reward an' all I get for my night's work is a black eye.

CURTIS. *(Sympathetically)* I'm sorry, Officer, but I was compelled to hit you. You were delaying me and I was afraid I'd lose The Phantom. However, I'll see that you are taken care of.

JERRY. *(Anxiously)* You mean it?

MRS. BLAKE. *(Indignantly)* Of course he means it. Can't you take a gentleman's word of honor, Officer?

ELEVEN. *(Crossing to* L. *of* JERRY) If dat White Phantom am in de hoosegow, who wuz de ghostes what spoke tuh me right here in dis very room?

JERRY. *(Impatiently)* You just imagined that.

ELEVEN. Imagined nothin'. Ah didn't imagine dat Ah turned all colors o' de rainbow, did Ah?

JERRY. *(Impatiently)* Now look here, Fifteen—

CURTIS. *(Interrupting him quickly)* The girl is right. She was speaking to somebody who was impersonating The White Phantom.

ETHAN. *(Bewilderedly)* But how could that be, Curtis?

CURTIS. *(Smiling at him)* Very easily, Mr. Sharp,

as I will demonstrate to you. *(Bends over and whispers in* MARION'S *ears. She nods in assent, crosses and exits* L.)

MRS. FRAZIER. *(Astonishedly)* Then it wasn't The White Phantom who was responsible for all of the disturbances in this house, son?

CURTIS. *(Emphatically)* No, indeed. You see, Officer, I've been too busy trying to land The White Phantom to pay much attention to the happenings here. But tonight I discovered the real cause of the shots and the other annoyances that have been going on in this house.

MRS. BLAKE. *(Rising; anxiously)* Who was it, Curt? Do tell us. The suspense is terrible.

ETHAN. *(Smiling at* CURTIS*)* Yes, let's have it, Frazier. I'd like to know who the guilty party is.

CURTIS. *(To* JERRY; *sternly)* Officer, the man who impersonated The White Phantom is standing beside you. Arrest Ethan Sharp and I'll prefer charges against him.

ETHAN. *(Indignantly)* This is ridiculous! You've nothing against me, Frazier!

MARION. *(As she enters quickly* L., *carrying a large white sheet and a pair of white cotton gloves)* I found the things just where you said I would, Curt.

CURTIS. *(Happily)* That's fine. Give them to the Officer. (ELEVEN *takes over to front of barrel.)*

MARION. *(Crosses up and hands the sheet and the gloves to* JERRY*)* Here you are, Officer. *(Stands* L. *of* JERRY.)

CURTIS. *(To* ETHAN; *sternly)* The game is up, Sharp! I can prove that you used those gloves and that sheet to impersonate The Phantom.

ELEVEN. *(Scratching the side of her head)* Ah done thought Ah'd heerd dat voice some place. Now Ah knows it. Dat's de ghostes what liked tuh scared me to death right in dis very room.

ETHAN. *(Trying to bluff it out)* This joke has gone far enough. I'il be at my office in the morning if you wish to see me, Officer. *(Wheels suddenly and starts for arch. JERRY reaches out his arm and grasps him by the shoulder.)*

CURTIS. *(Crossing to R. of ETHAN)* I know why you were so anxious to get all the tenants out of this house, Sharp. (MARION *crosses to* L. *of* MRS. BLAKE.)

JERRY. *(Examining the gloves)* These gloves are just like the ones I found in your pocket, Mr. Frazier.

CURTIS. *(Nodding in assent)* Of course. And I found those on the floor of this house the other night just after two pistol shots had been fired. I waited outside in the dark and saw Ethan Sharp leave the house.

MRS. BLAKE. *(Amazedly)* But why did he want the house kept empty?

CURTIS. I'll tell you. As you know, this house is part of the old Kingsley Estate. The remaining Kingsely heirs are so poor they can't pay the taxes on this place.

MRS. FRAZIER. *(Bewilderedly)* But why should Mr. Sharp—

CURTIS. *(Breaking in on her quickly)* I'll tell you, Mother. Sharp here conceived the brilliant idea of keeping the place vacant. If the Kingsley heirs didn't get any rent money they wouldn't be able to pay the taxes. The house would be put up for sale for back taxes and Sharp could buy it in for a song.

JERRY. *(Tightening his grip on* ETHAN'S *shoulder)* Pretty sharp, I'll say.

ETHAN. *(Realizing that he is trapped)* I didn't intend to harm anybody, Officer. It was all done in fun.

ELEVEN. *(Angrily)* Am dat what yuh all calls

fun? Ah kin still feel mah heart receedin' from mah mouth.

MRS. BLAKE. *(Bewilderedly)* I can't understand it yet. Where was Mr. Sharp when those shots were fired?

ETHAN. *(Nervously)* If I give you a complete confession will you promise to let me off easy, Officer?

JERRY. *(Threateningly)* I ain't promisin' nothin'. You're the one what's answerin' questions, not me. Where were you hidin' after them shots were fired?

ETHAN. *(Nervously)* Why—er—in the dumb-waiter. You never thought to look there for me. You see, it has a snap lock and I am the only person who has the key.

CURTIS. *(Smilingly)* You mean you *were* the only person— I had a key made for that dumb-waiter this afternoon. That's where Marion found the sheet and the pair of gloves.

MRS. BLAKE. *(In puzzled tones)* What about the telephone? One minute it rang and the next minute it was dead.

ETHAN. *(Nervously)* Why—er—that was very simple. After the telephone rang, I cut the wire on the outside. That's why you couldn't get Central.

CURTIS. *(Smiling at her)* You needn't be afraid to move into the house in the morning, Mrs. Blake. Mr. Sharp won't bother you again.

JERRY. *(Loudly)* I'll say he won't. Come along, you. *(Leads ETHAN to arch)* Don't forget your promise, Mr. Frazier. I'll be seein' you.

MRS. BLAKE. *(Crossing to L. of JERRY; curiously)* How much time will that Sharp man get, Officer?

JERRY. *(Importantly)* I don't know, but I mean to find out! *(Exits C. to R., with ETHAN.)*

MRS. BLAKE. *(Standing in arch Center)* I never did trust that Sharp man. I suspected him of being a villain the first time I ever laid eyes on him.

ELEVEN. *(Crossing to her; anxiously)* Does Ah hafta clean dis house now, Mis' Blake, ma'am?

MRS. BLAKE. *(Resolutely)* I should say not. I wouldn't move into this place if they gave it to me.

CURTIS. *(Crossing to* MARION*)* Perhaps we'll take it after we come back from our honeymoon, eh, Marion?

MRS. FRAZIER. *(Crossing to* R. *of* MRS. BLAKE*)* That's a splendid idea. Don't you think so, *dear* Mrs. Blake?

MRS. BLAKE. *(Beaming at her)* Simply divine, Anastasia. I always did want to see our children married to each other. *(WARN Curtain.)*

MRS. FRAZIER. *(Cordially)* Do come over and join my guests. That is, providing any of them are left.

MRS. BLAKE. *(Placing an arm around her waist; affectionately)* I'd love to. Come along, children. *I'll* have your entire wedding and honeymoon planned before the evening is over. *(Turning to* MRS. FRAZIER*)* You know, Anastasia, I always felt that Curt would make his mark in this world. Ten thousand dollars! I can hardly believe it! *(They laugh heartily and exit* C. *to* R.*)*

CURTIS. *(Taking* MARION's *hand)* Just think, Marion. We owe all our happiness to The White Phantom! *(They laugh happily and start for arch.)*

ELEVEN. (L. *of them; anxiously)* Jist a minute, Mis' Marion.

MARION. *(Pausing with* CURTIS *and facing* ELEVEN*)* What is it, Eleven?

ELEVEN. *(Curiously)* Den dey wuzn't nc real ghostes arter all?

MARION. *(Positively)* Of course not.

ELEVEN. *(Disappointedly)* Kin yuh beat dat? Ah turned all dem colors fer nothin'. Now Ah kain't even say dat Ah seed a real ghostes. Ah's regusted, dat's what Ah is.

CURTIS. *(Smiling at her)* Don't you worry about that, Eleven. After we're married you can come to work for us. Miss Marion and I are going to *haunt* each other for life. *(They ALL laugh happily as the Curtain falls.)*

END OF PLAY.

"THE WHITE PHANTOM"

PROPERTY PLOT

Two wooden boxes large enough to sit on, one Right
of Center, the other Left of Center.
A large sized empty barrel upstage, Left of arch
Center.
Telephone, connected to a long green cord, on floor
in upper Right corner.
Doorbell ring offstage, outside of arch Right.
Revolver (practical) with four shots (ETHAN).
Large white sheet with holes slit in the top to see
through; a pair of white cotton gloves (ETHAN).
Letter in a sealed envelope that ETHAN brings on
from off Left and places on top of fireplace.
Empty pail and a few cleaning cloths (ELEVEN).
Large chiffon handkerchief (MRS. FRAZIER).
A pair of white cotton gloves in CURTIS'S trouser
pocket.
The same white sheet and the pair of white cotton
gloves that ETHAN has worn and that MARION
brings on from off Left and hands to JERRY.

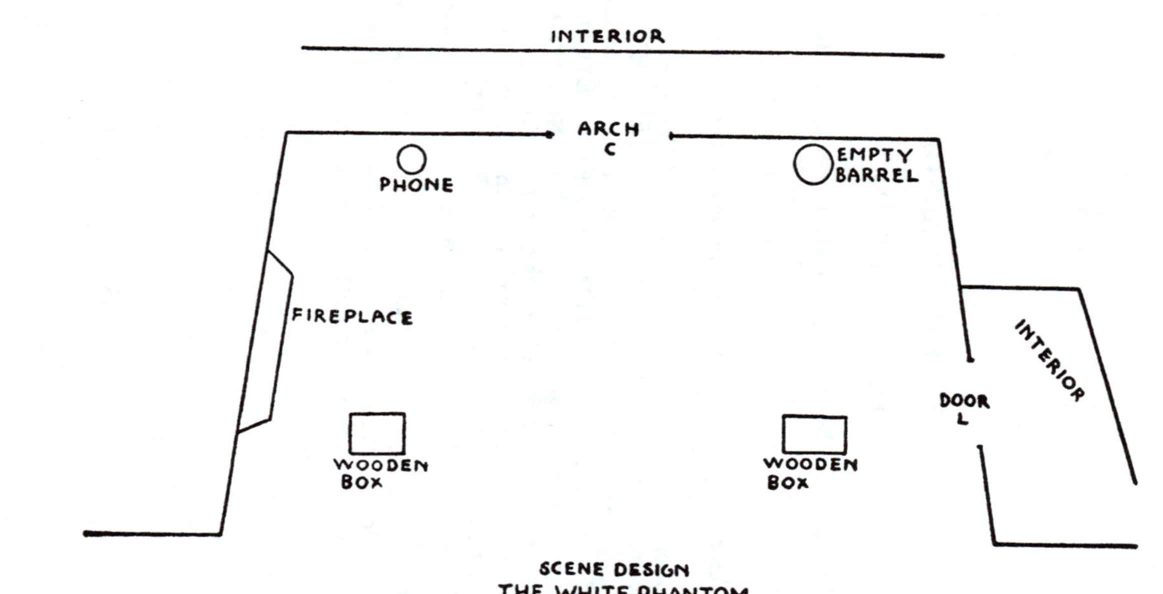

SCENE DESIGN
THE WHITE PHANTOM

DRACULA
Hamilton Deane and John L. Balderston

Drama / 6m, 2f / 3 Interiors

An enormously successful revival of this classic opened on Broadway in 1977, fifty years after the original production. This is one of the great mystery thrillers and is generally considered among the best of its kind. Lucy Seward, whose father is the doctor in charge of an English sanitorium, has been attacked by some mysterious illness. Dr. Van Helsing, a specialist, believes that the girl is the victim of a vampire, a sort of ghost that goes about at night sucking blood from its victims. The vampire is at last found to be a certain Count Dracula, whose ghost is at last laid to rest in a striking and novel manner. The play is intended for all who love thrills in the theater.

"Pure escape and great fun."
– *New York Post*

"An evening of high class fun."
– *Newsweek*

www.ingramcontent.com/pod-product-compliance
Lightning Source LLC
Chambersburg PA
CBHW070421120726
47909CB00005B/1739